ST. DAVID'S DAY IS CANCELLED!

ST. DAVID'S DAY IS CANCELLED!

Wendy White

Illustrated by Huw Aaron

Gomer

First published in 2017
by Gomer Press, Llandysul, Ceredigion SA44 4JL
www.gomer.co.uk

ISBN: 978 1 78562 208 3

A CIP record for this title is available from the British Library.

This book is published with the financial support
of the Welsh Books Council.

Printed and bound in Wales at
Gomer Press, Llandysul, Ceredigion

Chapter 1

Seren Wen and Me

About Us

I'm Seren Wen Rees. Rees is my family name and Seren is my first name. Wen is my middle name, but it somehow got stuck to my first name so that everyone calls me Seren Wen. It's Welsh and kind of means 'Bright Star'. And that's a lot to live up to – especially if you're me.

I've got a brother. He's my twin. He's got a regular name. He's called Dylan Rees. His middle name is Siôn but no one ever calls him that. Sometimes I call him Dylan Siôn, but mostly I just call him Dylan.

We're in the same class in school and we run the class newspaper.

About Our Newspaper

I'm the Editor and Agony Aunt, and Dylan comes up with lots of ideas for stories. He puts together the letters page as

well. Four other people help us too – Jac draws the illustrations and does the printing, Lucy makes

quizzes and crosswords, Nia takes photos and interviews people, and Rob is our sleuth. Yes, that's it, sleuth. It's a weird word I know, but Rob insists on using it.

It means he's a sort of detective. He wants to be a detective when he's older, but for now he's practising by listening to teachers in the corridors. He hears some amazing things.

When I came up with the idea of a newspaper we all tried to think of a name for it. After a lot

of not very original ideas, Nia suggested *Seren Wen*. Everyone thought it would be a good name for a paper. Everyone except me. And my brother, of course. But Dylan and I couldn't think of a better one. So Seren Wen is *my* name, and it's the name of our newspaper too.

How We Came to Save Saint David's Day

It all began with our head teacher, Mrs Right. We all think that Mrs Right is a good name for a head teacher. Well, you can't ever tell your head teacher she's wrong, can you? And most of the time she *is* right. She's OK really. But sometimes she's most definitely Mrs Wrong.

One morning, Rob our sleuth heard Mrs Right muttering something in the corridor. She wasn't muttering to anyone else, just to herself.

We're used to that. She does it a lot. I forgot to tell you that she can be a bit scatty.

At break time Rob called the *Seren Wen* team together to give us his report. Everyone was there – Dylan, Jac, Nia, Lucy and me. We were round the corner near the little shed where we keep the tools for the school's vegetable patch. It's where we always meet to discuss our stories.

'At oh eight hundred hours and fifty-three minutes this morning,' Rob began, 'I was standing in the corridor. Mrs Right, our head teacher, came out of the staffroom. I bent down and pretended to tie my shoe-laces.'

Rob Our Sleuth

I should warn you that Rob talks like this a lot. He thinks it's how detectives talk. Our dad's a detective. He doesn't talk like Rob. But the *Seren Wen* team are used to Rob, so we waited for him to get to the point.

'She was muttering in a worried manner,' he said. 'This is what she muttered, "If they're not going to make an effort this year, why not cancel it?" That's exactly what she said.'

'What's she going to cancel?' we all asked.

Rob looked down at his notepad. 'I followed Mrs Right to her office where she stopped and turned around. "Can I help you with anything, Robert?" she asked me.' Rob looked up at us.

'What did you say?' I asked.

He looked at his notes again. 'I replied, "No, Miss", upon which … she slammed her door.'

Chapter 2

What Happened Next

What Did Happen Next?

We all groaned and looked at each other in horror. What could it be? Mrs Right had cancelled a disco the term before because someone in our class had left all the taps in the toilets running – at full blast. We had our suspicions it had been Sneaky Sandra.

Sneaky Sandra

Rob had tried to use his sleuthing skills to find out who had left the taps running. But as it had happened in the *girls'* toilets he couldn't hang around there pretending to tie his shoe-laces. So we never found out for sure if it was Sandra or not.

But if something like that happens it's usually because of Sneaky Sandra or her equally sneaky friend Sid. They hate  our newspaper and they don't

 like us much either. And they're always doing things that spoil it for everyone else in class. Like talking when Sir has said, 'The next person to talk will keep the whole class in at break time'. You know the sort of person. Our mum says there's usually one in every class.

And she should know.

Our Mum

Our mum is a teacher. I think she's probably quite a nice teacher. I don't know for sure though, because she's never taught me and she doesn't work in our school. But she's a good mum to me and Dylan. She's always fair and she doesn't shout. Well, not often. And it must be hard for her not to shout at us because we can be very annoying sometimes. She gets tired working in school all day and looking after us all night. She doesn't get any help except from Gran. And from Dad every other weekend.

Back to Rob the Sleuth

'What do you think Mrs Right's going to cancel?' I asked Rob. 'There isn't a disco planned until next Christmas.' I was worried that we'd missed something. 'What could be happening? We always know everything that's going on.'

It was true. Our newspaper is so popular that we get to hear about every school trip, craft fair and cake sale. People want us to advertise events in *Seren Wen*, so we're always first to know.

'I can't believe something's about to be cancelled,' I said. 'And we've got no idea what it is.'

Rob held up his hand for me to be quiet.

'Before Mrs Right closed her door, I saw a calendar on her office wall. There was some writing on it. The writing said ...'

We all waited for Rob to carry on.

He always took absolutely ages to report anything to us. For a moment it looked like he was going to shut his notepad. But instead he turned over a page.

'The writing on the calendar said "St. David's Day",' he told us. 'And it was written on the square for Friday, the first of March.'

'Well, no surprises there,' said my brother. 'Saint David's Day is on

the first of March every year. So what?' And he put his basketball on his lap and wheeled off.

That's typical of Dylan. He can be a bit blunt sometimes.

Dylan and the Unicorns

Dylan used to be the Agony Aunt for the newspaper until somebody wrote to him about a wish they'd made on their last birthday. The person wanted to know if Dylan thought the wish might come true. Dylan's answer was printed in *Seren Wen*. It said, no, he didn't think their wish would ever come true. Because unicorns didn't exist. So they would NEVER own one as a pet, and they'd better get used to it.

Emily Sugarland cried for days afterwards. And Sir said I should be Agony Aunt instead of Dylan in future.

My Brother

By the way, Dylan uses a wheelchair to get around because his spine didn't grow like mine when we were babies. His chair doesn't have a motor or anything fancy like that, but it does have a Welsh dragon on the back. It looks really good. And because it hasn't got a motor, Dylan powers it with his arms, so they're pretty strong.

Punctuation Matters?

Like I said, Dylan picked up his basketball and started wheeling away. Nia, Jac and Lucy were about to follow him when Rob said, 'Don't you want to know what else Mrs Right had written?'

Dylan stopped. 'Go on then. But be quick. Break will be over soon.'

'In the same box as she'd written "Saint David's Day",' Rob said, 'she'd also put ...' He paused. We all waited.

'Just tell us, Rob,' I sighed.

'A question mark,' he said.

Chapter 3

The Question Mark

Thinking the Unthinkable

That question mark changed everything.
Dylan put down his basketball again and we
all grouped quietly in a circle. There was only
one thing that question mark could mean – Mrs
Right was thinking of cancelling Saint David's
Day. It was unbelievable. It was unthinkable.

It was unthinkable that she could even think it. But she must have been thinking it, because what else could the question mark mean?

We had to do something. But what?

Deciding What to Do

Nobody moved. Nobody spoke. We all just looked at the ground.

'We should say something to Mrs Right,' Dylan said eventually. 'We should ask her why she's cancelled Saint David's Day.'

'But we don't know for sure she *has* cancelled it,' I said. 'The question mark just means she's *thinking* of cancelling it. And we'd have to admit that Rob sneaked a look at her calendar. You know she doesn't like him snooping round her office.'

Everyone nodded. Mrs Right had caught Rob sneaking a look inside her office once too often. 'Next time I catch you being nosy,' she'd told him the week before, 'I'll ban you from the corridors at playtime.'

We couldn't have that. We needed him to sleuth for us.

'I could just stand outside her door,' Rob suggested, 'and accidentally listen in on her conversations.'

'Oh no,' we all said at once.

'Sooner or later she'd catch you,' Dylan said. 'And then how would we manage without our sleuth?' Everyone nodded again. Rob just shrugged.

'There's only one thing we can do,' I said. 'We'd better talk to Sir.'

Sir

I meant to tell you about Sir sooner. He's our class teacher and his real name is Mr Morgan, but we all just call him Sir. He's a good teacher – you know the sort, kind, cheerful and patient. He's very

accident-prone, pretty short-sighted and he's always hungry too.

He only gets angry when he really needs to and he's strict but fair. I know it doesn't seem fair to keep us all in at break time because of Sneaky Sandra and Sneaky Sid, but you know what it's like – sometimes he has to.

Peer Pressure

Dylan did some research for the newspaper and he found out it's called 'peer pressure'. Sandra and Sid are meant to feel sorry for behaving badly and keeping us in at break. They're meant to pick up on our disappointment. We're over half way through the year now and they're still not picking up on it. You can't blame Sir though. He's tried everything else.

Crime and Punishment

The first week of term, when Sandra and Sid wouldn't stop talking in class, he sent them outside to litter pick. Somehow they managed to make the playground even messier than it was before. Next he gave them one hundred lines each. But when Sir's back was turned, Sandra forced Sid to write hers too.

And when he tried setting them extra spelling homework, Sneaky Sandra's mother rang him up. She said it was obvious he didn't care about children's human rights, and if he gave out extra homework again she would be consulting her solicitor.

Poor Sir. When it comes to Sneaky Sandra and Sneaky Sid he just can't win.

But the rest of our class think he's great. He's what Gran likes to call 'approachable'. So that's what I did – I approached him.

Chapter 4

The Note

What Sir Said

After the bell had rung and we'd all lined up
and trooped into class, I went up to Sir's desk.
He was reading a note and shaking his head.
'Dear me,' he kept saying. 'Dear, dear me.'

I didn't like to interrupt him, so I just waited
by his desk. He didn't seem to notice me. That's
something I forgot to tell you about him. Sir's
often in a world of his own. He can stare out of
the window for a whole hour at a time.

'This is terrible,' he said. He was still holding
the paper. He was still shaking his head. 'In all
my time as a teacher ...' He suddenly looked up.
'Oh, Seren Wen! I didn't see you there. Are you
alright?'

'Yes, Sir,' I said. Then I noticed his cheeks were bright pink. 'Are you?'

Sir shook his head. Then he nodded his head. Then he shook his head again. Finally he said, 'It's just this note from Mrs Right.' And he made a loud growling sound as if he was very cross. We're used to Sir's strange sounds. He makes quite a lot of them.

Suddenly he scrunched up the piece of paper and threw it into the bin. Then he looked at me again. 'What did you want, Seren Wen?' he asked

in his normal voice.
It was as if he hadn't
been growling two
seconds before.

'I wanted to ask
you about Saint David's Day, Sir,' I said. 'We
were wondering if we should advertise the
concert in the class paper.'

Sir's pink cheeks got even pinker. He started
looking at me oddly. 'Seren Wen, are you a
mind reader?'

'I don't think so, Sir,' I said. But then I
remembered something.

Chicken Pie

I don't really believe I can read minds. Not
really. Not *really*.

But sometimes I like to think I can. And then
I somehow convince myself that I can actually
do it. And sometimes I can convince other people
that I can do it too. Like Dylan.

We like asking each other to guess things –
you know, all that *twins always know what the other
one's thinking* rubbish. And our guesses are always
wrong, so that's OK.

But one day, Dylan asked me to guess what
he'd had for dinner at his friend Kieran's house.

'Chicken pie,' I said straight away, and Dylan's
mouth fell open.

Gran was going
past with a basketful
of dirty clothes at the
time. She looked at
Dylan's mouth. 'You
could drive a bus into that,' she said, and she
carried on her way to the washing machine.

'How … how did you know?' Dylan finally
managed to say.

To be honest with you, I don't know how I
knew. But I wasn't going to tell him that. 'I can
read your mind, of course, Dylan Siôn,' I said.

To tell you the truth, chicken pie had just

popped into my head. He's never told me he's had it at Kieran's house before. We hadn't had it at home for ages. Or at school. But that's what was in my head, so that's what I said. And I was right. It was my first guess too, and he'd given me three.

Dylan's usually quite cynical. That's another one of Gran's words. It means he doesn't believe things very easily. Especially if it involves his sister – that means me. But he looked at me in a strange way, like he was a bit proud of me. He's never normally proud of me. And since then he's been very careful what he thinks around me. Especially if it involves food.

But Back to Sir

Sir was still looking at me oddly. Then he smiled. 'No, of course you're not a mind reader. But how else could you know? Mrs Right told us teachers not to tell anyone.' He rubbed his chin. 'Saint David's Day,' he said. 'Funny you should mention that, Seren Wen …'

He tapped his pen on his desk. Then he tapped it on his head. He's always doing that. Sometimes he forgets it's on and he ends up with ink dots all over his forehead.

'No comment!' he said suddenly.

I wasn't sure I had heard him properly. 'Sorry Sir?'

'I have no comment to make about Saint David's Day,' he said. 'Now go back to your desk, Seren Wen.' And then he told us all to open our Maths books.

Wet Play

By lunchtime it had started to rain. You know what it's like, wet play and all that. At first it's fun being in class and not having to do any work. Then everyone starts to get bored. And they get noisy. Then the dinner supervisors get cross. And finally your head teacher has to come in and tell you all to 'BE QUIET!'

Anyway, this wet lunchtime was great news for the *Seren Wen* team, because we had a dilemma.

The Dilemma

Our lunchtime dilemma was this – should we take the note out of the bin or not? You remember the note, don't you? The one Sir threw away just before I asked him about Saint David's Day. And just after he'd said 'Dear, dear me'.

'We can't just take something out of the bin,' Lucy said. 'It doesn't seem right.'

'I think we can,' said Dylan. 'I've had to take work out of the bin before. And Sir told me to do it, remember?'

We did. Dylan can get a bit hotheaded

sometimes. Especially with long division. One day he ripped a page out of his Maths book and threw it in the bin. None of us had forgotten how cross Sir had been.

'That was different,' Lucy said. 'This could be called snooping. And Mrs Right might come in and catch us.'

'Everyone's getting very noisy too,' Jac said. 'She might come in any minute now.' He turned to me. 'What do you think we should do, Seren Wen?'

Then the whole *Seren Wen* team looked at me.

Chapter 5

The Miracle

Sensible Me?

I haven't told you this before because it's a bit embarrassing, but the *Seren Wen* team think I'm sensible. They do, honest! Well, maybe not Dylan. But Nia, Jac, Lucy and Rob do. They think I'm good in a dilemma. I'm not at all sensible. Really I'm not. But they won't listen.

'Don't look at me,' I said. 'I don't know what we should do.'

'You *are* the Agony Aunt,' Lucy insisted. 'You're supposed to know what to do in a difficult situation.'

'No one's ever asked me if they should take something out of a bin before now,' I said.

It was true. I get lots of letters about falling out with friends, but I've never had one about bins.

Rob cleared his throat. 'In my expert opinion, looking at that piece of paper could not be called snooping. The paper in question is in a public place.' He waved his arms around at our classroom. 'We are within our rights to extract that note from the wastepaper basket.'

'I don't know,' I said. 'It still feels kind of wrong to go looking through the bin.'

And then a miracle happened.

Those Sneakies Again

OK, so it wasn't really a miracle. It was Sneaky Sandra's foot kicking a pencil case. That's typical of her. She loves kicking things around in class. She loves doing anything that's not allowed. And of course Sneaky Sid was there too saying, 'Kick it, Sandra. Kick it!'

The pencil case flew up into the air and scattered pens and pencils everywhere. Sneaky

Sid cheered and clapped his hands as if it were the cleverest thing ever. Then the pencil case came down onto a pile of Maths books. Sir had dumped the books on the edge of a table as he was running for dinner. He really did run for dinner – it was pizza and salad, his favourite. So he didn't put the books down in a proper pile. It was all higgledy-piggledy. And it was pretty wobbly too. When the pencil case hit them, the books slid all over the table and crashed onto the floor.

The Sneakies doubled over laughing because sitting at that desk was Emily Sugarland. She was quietly colouring a picture of some mermaids. You remember Emily, don't you? She's the person who cried for a week because Dylan told her unicorns didn't exist. Well, Emily had a terrible fright when the pile of books fell over. She thought something was attacking her. She jumped up at once, flapping her arms about. She was shaking her feet too, and one of them knocked over the bin.

Yes, that bin. The one with the note in it.

All the rubbish inside the bin fell out. We couldn't believe our luck!

Rob Steps In

Sneaky Sandra and Sneaky Sid were laughing so much they had fallen onto their knees. They were making a lot of noise. Emily looked at the floor. There were pens, books and waste paper everywhere. 'Oh dear,' she said. 'What a mess.'

Emily Sugarland is very neat, with very neat hair and very neat writing. She even keeps all her pens in order. She has a different pencil case for each type. She has one for metallic, one for scented and another for sparkly pens.

Anyway, Emily put down her pen – it was a sparkly one – and rushed to tidy up the papers that had fallen out of  the bin. Suddenly Rob leapt into action.

'Stop what you are doing at once, Miss Sugarland,' he said in his best detective voice.

But at that moment, Mrs Right appeared at the classroom door. Yes, that Mrs Right. Our head teacher.

Chapter 6

Rocks

Mrs Right – Again

'What's going on here?' Mrs Right asked.

Everyone suddenly stopped what they were doing. We became very quiet. She looked at all the pens, pencils and books on the floor. Then she saw the knocked-over bin. And next to the bin were Emily and Rob.

'Did you knock that over?' she asked. She was looking right at Rob, and she didn't look too friendly.

Out of the corner of my eye I saw the Sneakies crawling into a dark corner as quickly as they could.

'It wasn't Rob,' Emily said. 'It was me. I knocked over the bin because those books jumped across my desk – *by magic.*' Trust Emily to bring magic into it.

Mrs Right ignored her. She was still looking at Rob. 'You seem to be everywhere I turn, Robert Roberts. Get that mess cleared up at once.'

It was just the chance he needed. Rob held a hand to his head and saluted her. 'At your service, Mrs Right. I'll jump to it.' And he began picking up the papers. He glanced quickly at each one before stuffing them back into the bin.

I saw him slip one paper very carefully into his pocket.

Mrs Right hadn't noticed. She gave the whole class a long last look. 'Keep the noise down,' she said, and with that the bell to end lunchtime rang and Sir came back into class.

The Long, Long Wait

The afternoon dragged and dragged. The whole *Seren Wen* team was desperate to look at the note Rob had put in his pocket. We kept trying to catch his eye across the classroom. Had he read it under the desk when Sir wasn't looking? Had he? *Had he?* It was impossible to tell. Rob's face was totally blank. He's good at having a blank face. He says he'll need it when he's a detective and has to interview criminals.

I was really, *really* desperate to slide over to Rob's desk and ask him about the note. I wanted to read it for myself too. And on any other day I could have just gone over to have a quick chat with Rob. Sir wouldn't mind. He lets us have a little chat now and again, so long as we don't talk too much. Or too loudly. But today I couldn't because, unfortunately, we had to watch one of Sir's geography films.

Sir's Films

Normally I love Sir's geography films. He draws the blinds in class and you can put your head on your desk and fall asleep in the dark without him noticing. It's easy to fall asleep too – you just have to listen to Sir's voice going on and

on and on. He says things like: 'This is the hill I slipped down in the Lake District', or 'This is the river I fell into in the Cotswolds'. Today's film was about him climbing Snowdon.

'This,' he said, when a stony path came up on the screen, 'is where I broke my ankle.' We all nodded. We remembered Sir breaking his ankle. He was in plaster for weeks.

Sir's film was OK, I suppose. And Snowdon looked very nice with snow on the top and everything, but I was itching to ask Rob about the note. I was so worked up about it I couldn't fall asleep, not even when Sir said, 'And now

here are some fascinating rocks I saw when I was waiting to be airlifted off the mountain.'

40

'Did you film the rescue helicopter, Sir?' Jac asked excitedly. And we all lifted our heads from our desks and sat up straight. For once it looked like Sir's film might get interesting.

'Unfortunately,' Sir said, 'my video camera ran out of battery charge just before the helicopter arrived. There were so many fascinating rocks to film, you see. Like this one for example ...'

We silently groaned and slumped back onto our desks. The rocks didn't look very fascinating to me. In fact, I could have sworn that Sir had just filmed the same rock over and over again. We all sighed with relief when the bell rang for home time, and we shot out of class like a stampede of greyhounds.

Chapter 7

What the Note Said

The Shock

The *Seren Wen* team met by the tool shed. Once we'd checked that the Sneakies weren't spying on us, Rob took the note from his pocket.

'Have you read it?' we all asked.

'I have indeed checked its contents covertly while Mr  Morgan was otherwise engaged,' Rob said. Which meant he'd read the note under the desk while Sir was looking the other way.

 'What does it say?' we all asked him.

He shook his head. His face was very serious. 'It's just as we feared. Saint David's Day has been cancelled.'

And even though we'd all expected it, we still had quite a shock.

Panic! Panic!

'How can Mrs Right do that to us? It's so unfair!' Dylan shouted.

I was just about to tell him to keep his voice down, when I saw

Mrs Right's little red car zooming out through the school gates.

'You are correct, Dylan,' Rob said. 'It *is* unfair.' We all nodded. We couldn't believe it. How could it be true? How could she be cancelling our national day?

'What *exactly* did the note say?' I asked Rob.

He opened the piece of paper. He had folded it up into a tiny square. 'Just in case I had to hide it in my sock,' he told us. We'd all got a whiff of Rob's socks in PE that morning. We were glad he hadn't had to hide the note there. He opened it up and began to read.

Could We Be More Shocked?

'"Just a quick note to all the staff",' he read in his detective-style voice, '"to let you know that there will be no Saint David's Day celebrations this year. That terrible concert we had last year was the final straw. No one in the junior classes bothered to wear a Welsh costume, and most of

44

them didn't even wear a daffodil or leek. Only two people tried to learn a poem – and they both forgot their lines half way through. And as for the dreadful singing! A choir of cats with belly ache would have been more tuneful. So I'm giving up. It will be classes as usual this year."' Rob looked up at our shocked faces. 'Classes as usual. That's what she says.'

'She can't do that,' Lucy said.

Jac shook his head. 'It's just not right.'

'We've got to stop her,' Dylan said.

'But how?' asked Nia.

'I've got an idea,' I heard myself say. And everyone turned to look at me.

Sensible Me

To be honest, I'd kind of had this idea ever since Rob told us about the question mark. You remember the question mark, don't you? The one Mrs Right had written on her calendar. I'd been planning what to do if she cancelled Saint David's Day since then. After all, the first of March was next Friday. I had to start planning because we didn't have much time.

OK, so sometimes I *can* be sensible.

'We've got to get everyone interested in putting on a really good concert,' I said. 'Everyone. The whole school.'

'But how can we?' Dylan asked. He was scuffing the wheels of his chair one way then the other. He always does that when he's fed up. 'Saint David's Day has been cancelled, remember?'

'The teachers know it's been cancelled,' I said, 'but no one's told us. Sir didn't give us a letter to

46

take home today, did he? And Mrs Right hasn't called one of her "special assemblies".'

'No, you're right,' Nia said. 'She hasn't, thank goodness.'

Mrs Right's Special Assemblies

What can I say about Mrs Right's special assemblies? You know when a head teacher gets really, really excited about something and they want you to get really, really excited about it too? They go on and on about it in a long assembly. And they do strange voices. And they jump up and down

a lot. And sometimes, if you're very unlucky, they burst into song. And then, if you're very, *very* unlucky, they dance too. Well, that's what Mrs Right does in her special assemblies. *Every single one.*

But Back to the Playground

'How could she do a special assembly about cancelling something?' Jac asked. 'It's hard to get excited about that.'

'She'd manage it somehow,' Nia said.

'Well, we'd better be quick before she does.' I looked at them all. 'We've got to get everyone signed up to do something tomorrow.'

'But tomorrow will be too late,' Dylan said. He was still scuffing his wheels. 'She'll call an

 assembly first thing in the morning, before we've even had a chance to talk to the people in our own class, let alone the whole school.'

He was right. She always held her assemblies at nine o'clock. On the dot. There would be no time to put our plan into operation the next morning.

We all looked very glum.

Chapter 8

Rob to the Rescue

Our Super Sleuth

Yes, everyone looked very glum – apart from Rob. He was grinning. He opened his notebook and cleared his throat.

'At exactly three o'clock twenty-two minutes today,' he began – he hadn't quite got to grips with the twenty-four hour clock yet – 'I was proceeding down the corridor in the general direction of the staffroom when I heard Mrs Right say, "I had better get my skates on or I'll be late for my computer course."'

I nodded. That made sense. I'd seen Mrs Right dashing off in her little red car, remember? And we all knew how much she needed computer training.

Mrs Right and her Computer

Mrs Right gets into a dreadful muddle every day with her computer. She's always running into our class shouting, 'Mr Morgan, come quick! I've just deleted everyone's end-of-year reports and I don't know how to get them back!' Or, 'Mr Morgan, come quick! I've just ordered ten thousand bags of cotton wool for the first aid box and I don't know how to cancel them!' Or something daft like that.

But the best muddle she ever got into was in the summer holidays, when Sir wasn't around to help her.

Mrs Right and her Face Pack

There were two new teachers starting in our school after the summer holidays, and Mrs Right wanted everyone to recognise them on their first day. So she emailed a photo of the new teachers to all the parents with the sentence: 'These are our two new members of staff – I'm sure you'll make them feel very welcome at the start of term.' It was a good idea, I suppose, except she muddled up her photos.

Instead of emailing a photo of the new teachers, she emailed a photo of her and her sister at the health spa. They like going to the health spa. They go there every Sunday afternoon – we know because Rob overheard her telling Miss Juno about it in the corridor one day.

The parents thought Mrs Right had decided to send out a very unusual picture, because the

two people in it were wearing bath robes and sitting next to a hot tub. But no one realised it was Mrs Right and her sister because their faces were covered in green face packs, and they had cucumber slices over their eyes.

On the first day of term it turned out that the two new teachers were men. Parents started asking who the ladies sitting around the hot tub were, so Mrs Right had to send out a letter to explain. She was very embarrassed and hasn't emailed any parents since.

Back to Rob

'So what if Mrs Right has got a computer course this afternoon?' Dylan said. He was itching to wheel away, I could tell. Another few seconds and he'd be gone. 'That's no help to us tomorrow.'

Rob looked at Dylan. 'Just a moment,' he said, and he flipped over a page of his notebook. 'Mrs Right ran from the staffroom …'

That's typical of Mrs Right too. She runs

everywhere, but if we so much as break into a trot she shouts 'Walk in the corridors, please!' and then she'll sprint off round a corner.

But back to Rob reading his notebook. '… and she was calling to Mr Morgan, "The course is carrying on tomorrow morning, so I won't be back in school until the afternoon."' Rob closed his notebook and looked at us all.

'Wow, Rob,' I said. 'You're the best sleuth ever.' And I grinned at him.

'I don't get it,' Jac said. 'How does Mrs Right going on a computer course help us save Saint David's Day?'

Dylan bounced his basketball hard at the wall and caught it again. 'I think you'll find,' he said, 'if our head teacher isn't in school tomorrow morning, we will have what our brilliant sleuth Rob would call "a window of opportunity".'

Rob nodded. He had a huge grin on his face. 'Exactly.'

But Jac still looked puzzled.

'We've got time to print the newspaper and give a copy to everyone in school after all,' I said. 'Tomorrow morning.'

Chapter 9

What We Did Next

Our Den

That evening we all went round to Nia's house. She lives in the centre of town so we always meet there. And she's got a shed at the bottom of her garden that her parents don't mind us using. It's a great place to sit around thinking up ideas.

Ages ago we put an old rug from my bedroom on the floor. And we brought an old beanbag from Dylan's room too. Jac and Lucy brought some big cushions that their mums didn't want any more. And Rob brought a periscope from his house and fixed it to the window. It's to check that Nia's little brothers don't sneak up on us and listen at the door. The shed's comfy and cosy. We love meeting there. We call it our den.

Storming Brains

'We need to brainstorm again,' I told everyone in the den. I like the idea of brainstorming, when so many things are going on in your brain, and someone else's brain too, that it makes a storm. I think it's a bit like shaking a snow globe. But instead of fake snow, there are lots of ideas floating around. And it's inside your head. It's brilliant!

Anyway everyone smiled at me. They're used to me saying 'brainstorm'. I say it a lot.

Dylan was sitting on the beanbag. 'We need good ideas,' he agreed. 'And lots of them. We've got to make this the best Saint David's Day ever. Otherwise Mrs Right might cancel it for always.'

We were quiet. We were thinking about what it would be like to never have Saint David's Day ever, ever again.

Eventually Lucy said, 'She wouldn't really do that, would she?'

'It's a distinct possibility, I'm afraid,' Rob said. More than any of us, Rob knows how hot-headed our head teacher can be. He's had more tellings-off from her than the rest of us put together. 'I think she might very well cancel it for good.'

'OK then.' I handed out paper and pens. 'We'd better start thinking. And fast.'

A Surprise for Sir

Next morning the *Seren Wen* team got to school early. We knew Sir would be already in class. He always arrives an hour before we do in the mornings. It's because he likes to plan the lessons for the day ahead and catch up on marking books. It's also because he likes to start the morning with a big mug of coffee and a quiet read of the daily newspaper. And that's what he was doing when we walked into class.

'H … h … hello,' he said, looking up from the sports pages to the clock on our classroom wall.

'Oh!' He put his hand on his chest. 'It's only quarter past eight.' He looked relieved. 'What are you all doing here so early?'

'We're on a mission, Sir,' Dylan said, tapping the stack of printer paper on his lap. 'We're going to save Saint David's Day.'

Sir Lets the Secret Slip

'Really?' Sir smiled. We could see from his face that he was impressed. And then he remembered something. 'Hang on, you're not supposed to know about that. Mrs Right hasn't told anyone but the staff that she's cancelling Saint David's Day.'

And then he stopped and slapped his hand over his mouth. 'I wasn't supposed to say that,' he  said from between his fingers. 'It was meant to be a secret until Mrs Right announces it in assembly tomorrow.'

'It's alright, Sir,' Dylan said.

'We won't tell her you told us. And it's probably best if we don't tell you how we found out about it in the first place.'

'Well,' Sir sighed, 'I'm very glad you did find out. The teachers are all really upset. None of us wants Saint David's Day cancelled, but no one can think of a way to change Mrs Right's mind. You know what she's like when she decides on something.'

And we certainly did.

Chapter 10

Mrs Right's Wrong Decisions

Fifty Pots of Paint

Sometimes Mrs Right makes up her mind very quickly. And once she's decided on something, a hundred hurricanes won't change her mind.

For instance, one day last term Mrs Right decided that the school needed brightening up. So she rang the local paint shop and asked if they had some spare paint. They did. They had fifty pots of green paint that no one else wanted. Our

 school could have them for fifty pence a pot. 'Thank you,' Mrs Right said. 'That'll be perfect.'

Lime Green?

When she got all fifty pots to school, Mr Morgan opened one of them. 'That looks very bright to me,' he said, and all the other teachers agreed with him.

'Perhaps we'd be better off with a nice shade of blue,' Mr Harry suggested.

'Or a lovely pale yellow,' said Mrs Candy.

'Or just leaving the walls the colour they are,' Mr Killer said.

But Mrs Right wouldn't listen to anyone. We know because Rob was outside in the corridor. And he overheard it all.

'Nonsense,' she said. 'That lime green is perfect. It's just what the classroom walls need.' And she spent the whole weekend painting every centimetre of the school.

Sunglasses – indoors!

On Monday morning we couldn't believe our eyes. The walls were hideous. Hid-*eeee*-ous! Mr Morgan had to wear sunglasses in class. He said the lime green walls were giving him terrible headaches. And all the other teachers started wearing sunglasses too. Then the children started. And in the end everyone was wearing sunglasses.

Everyone except Mrs Right. She kept saying the school looked wonderful and lime green was her favourite colour.

Then a few weeks later we arrived in school to find Mrs Right had spent the whole weekend painting the walls a lovely shade of blue. We were all very relieved.

But Back to Our Plan

'How, exactly, are you going to save Saint David's Day?' Sir asked.

I took out a piece of paper from my bag. 'We've got a plan.' I put the paper on Sir's desk. 'We're going  to print an article in *Seren Wen* called "The Best Saint David's Day Ever."' I pointed to the article I'd written the night before on the piece of paper. Sir squinted at it. As usual he couldn't read my handwriting. 'Don't worry,' I said. 'It'll make sense once I've typed it up. We're going to challenge everyone to think of something really exciting to do for the concert.'

'And we're going to have prizes,' Lucy said. 'For the best song, best poem and best dance.'

'And we're going to have a cookery competition too,' Jac said.

'And treats for everyone who wears a Welsh costume,' Nia added.

The brainstorming session we'd had the night before had been fantastic. We'd come up with so many ideas. We were very excited. We could do it. We could actually save Saint David's Day!

Sir scratched his head. 'That's an awful lot of prizes. Where are you getting them all from?'

And then our bubble burst.

Prizes?

We all looked at each other.

Dylan groaned. 'I guess we didn't think about how we'd actually get the prizes.'

'We can buy them,' Nia suggested.

'With what?' Lucy said. 'The last time I checked we had one pound fifty in *Seren Wen*'s

funds. And I'm not asking Mrs Right for any more money. Please,' she begged, turning to me, '*please* don't make me ask her.'

Mrs Money-Bags

I could understand why Lucy was begging. Mrs Right gives us a ten pound note at the start of each term to cover the cost of printer paper. And by the middle of term we've nearly always spent every penny – well, printer paper is pretty expensive and we use a lot of it. So Lucy has to ask for another tenner, because she's in charge of the money side of things. Then Mrs Right says 'Who do you think I am – Mrs Money-Bags?'

Lucy hates asking Mrs Right and Mrs Right hates handing over more money. She hates it so much that she makes Lucy explain exactly how we've spent the first ten pounds. *Exactly.* Down to the last penny. 'It's good practise for when you're an accountant,' she always tells Lucy. 'I want to be a vet,' Lucy says. 'Vets need money skills too,' Mrs Right says. You can never get the last word with her.

Back to the Prizes

'Don't worry,' I said to Lucy. 'We can't ask Mrs Right for money to buy prizes anyway, because then she'll know what we're up to.'

'But she'll know what you're up to anyway,' Sir pointed out, 'once she sees the article in *Seren Wen*.'

'Yes, Sir,' I said. 'That *would* be a problem – except I know something about Mrs Right that you don't ...'

Chapter 11

Making Fun of Mrs Right

Mrs Right's Secret

What I knew about Mrs Right was this – she never reads our newspaper. She pretends she's read every edition. She makes vague comments about how wonderful this or that article is. But it's obvious she doesn't know what she's talking about. I know it's ridiculous. She's our head teacher, after all. She *ought* to read the articles that we send out to all the classes. We could be writing absolutely anything. For all she knows, we could be plotting to take over the whole school.

We're not, of course, but what we *are* doing is much more fun. And it's all down to Jac.

Jac the Cartoonist

We really shouldn't make fun of our head teacher. No, I'm serious – we *really* shouldn't. But sometimes we just can't help it.

After she sent the wrong photo to our parents – the one of her and her sister in towels and face packs – it was very hard not to make just a bit of fun of her. We couldn't resist.

And Jac is *sooo* good at drawing. He drew this really very, *very* funny cartoon of her and her sister jumping into the hot tub. They had big white towels and green face packs, and gigantic feet and hands. And he drew the two new teachers – Mr Terry and Mr Killer – standing in the background with their hands over their eyes looking shocked.

When we saw Jac's cartoon we all agreed we just had to print it in *Seren Wen*. It was too good

not to. Everyone thought it would be great to make it huge, and we thought we should put it on the front page.

Sensible Me Again

But at the very last minute, just before we started printing, I got nervous – well, I am supposed to be the sensible one, remember? And I'm the editor too, so I get to make the final decision. I couldn't take Jac's cartoon out because it was much too funny to throw away. So I made it smaller and moved it to the middle page. And on the front page I put an article called "Safest Cycle Routes to School".

Once the newspaper had been printed, everyone was talking about Jac's cartoon. Even the teachers and parents. Everyone thought it was hilarious.

And then Mrs Right cornered me outside the staffroom. Oh no, I thought, I'm in for it now. But she was smiling at me sweetly. 'I really enjoyed your article about cycling to school, Seren Wen,' she told me. 'All those tips about which roads are safest.' She was still smiling. 'You're doing a great job with that newspaper. It's well worth ten pounds a term for the cost of printer paper.' Then she ran off down the corridor.

And since then Jac has drawn lots of hilarious cartoons of Mrs Right for *Seren Wen*. We always put them on the inside pages and she hasn't seen any of them. And that's how we know Mrs Right only ever looks at the front page of our newspaper.

Dylan's Idea

But back to the prizes. How could we get enough money together to buy them?

I was trying to do a quick brainstorm all by myself when Dylan suddenly said, 'Sir, will the teachers be pleased if we save Saint David's Day?' He'd obviously been doing some brainstorming of his own.

'Oh yes,' Sir said. 'They'll be jumping up and down on the staffroom chairs when I tell them about your plan.' Then he clamped his hand over his mouth again and looked at us. 'Forget I said that,' he whispered through his fingers. 'That thing about jumping on chairs.'

'Of course, Sir,' we all said, but I caught Jac's eye. I could tell he was already picturing how he

would draw that crazy staffroom scene. Sir was very good at letting things slip. He didn't know it, but he gave us most of our ideas for teasing the staff.

'Do you think the teachers might help us put our plan into operation?' Dylan asked.

'Certainly,' Sir said. 'I'm sure they'll help in any way they can.'

Dylan was smiling cheekily. I could tell he had a really good plan up his sleeve. He said, 'Do you think they might help us buy some prizes, Sir?'

Chapter 12

Putting Our Plan into Action

The Whip-round

'Prizes?' Sir repeated. He looked at us blankly.

Then he grinned and tapped his nose. 'I see what you mean, Dylan. I'm sure they'll help. I'll have a whip-round in the staffroom.' He got out his wallet from his pocket. 'And to start things off,' he said, taking out a five pound note, 'you can have this.' And he dropped it into his empty coffee mug. 'I'll go and see who's in the staffroom right now. They'll want to hear the good news.'

And with that, off he dashed.

'Thanks, Sir,' we called after him.

'Great idea, bro,' I said. My brother's very good at coming up with ideas just when you need them most. I grinned. 'Problem solved.'

Dylan shrugged. 'It's *part* of the problem solved,' he said. 'We've still got loads to do.'

'You're right.' I looked at the clock. Half past eight. That meant we had half an hour before school started. 'OK,' I said to the team, 'let's get to work. We haven't got much time.'

Action Stations

We settled down at the computers, got out the articles we'd written the night before and began typing. Our fingers flew over the keys. We were used to working to deadlines – we'd had lots of them since we'd started *Seren Wen* back in the

autumn – but this deadline was very tight. And it wasn't long before Sir came back into class ready for the start of lessons. He put down his mug on the table next to me. It was full of coins and notes.

'There's plenty there to buy all the prizes you need,' he said. 'The other teachers were only too happy to help. They think your plan to save Saint David's Day is wonderful.'

'Thanks, Sir,' I grinned at him quickly. I was still typing as fast as I could. 'That's brilliant. We'll get pens and books as prizes. The teachers will think that's a good way to spend their money.'

I glanced at the clock. It was almost time for the rest of our class to come in from the playground. We weren't going to make it. We still had too much to type up.

Sir saw my worried face. 'I've got creative writing planned for our first lesson,' he said. He looked at the six of us typing away madly. 'You've all been very creative already. So you

can carry on typing and get the paper finished.'

'Thanks, Sir,' I said again. And this time my grin was huge.

Phew!

By break time we had finished typing. Jac was feeding paper into the printer like it was some hungry metal monster.

Lucy, Nia and Dylan were busy checking and folding the printed papers, and Rob and I were counting out copies for each class.

'Nearly there,' I said. 'Just our class to go now.' I sat on the desk and picked up a copy of the paper.

The front page looked good. "School Meals We Love" the headline said, and below that was written "Roving reporter Nia Jeffries talks to pupils about their favourite school dinners". Nia had done a brilliant job of interviewing people all week, and she'd made a list of the meals they liked best. Pizza had come out on top – surprise, surprise!

'Mrs Right will take one look at that front page and be delighted,' I said to Rob. 'She won't look any further.' I turned to pages two and three. The headlines on these

 pages were huge. "Best Saint David's Day Ever" and "Win Prizes!" they shouted.

In the articles we asked everyone to try their very, *very* best to learn songs and poems for the concert. We told them we were running a baking competition to find the best Welsh cakes. And we explained that this year we needed to hold the most brilliant Saint David's Day *ever* – there were plenty of prizes on offer.

And we made it clear that it was all a big surprise for Mrs Right, so no one should mention it to her.

'I think that'll get our message across,' Rob said, glancing over my shoulder at the headlines. 'There we go.' He put one last copy onto the stack. 'All done.'

The Big Ask

We punched the air, patted each
other on the back – you know, all
the sorts of things you do when
you're really happy.

Except a bit of me wasn't feeling so great.
I was really pleased that we'd managed to get
all the copies printed in time. I was really, *really*
pleased. But I was a bit worried too. What if
our plan didn't work? We were asking a lot of
the rest of the school. What if nobody wanted
to learn songs and poems and put on a good
concert? What if the rest of the school just didn't
care?

Chapter 13

Worried Me

My Imaginings

Sometimes sensible me turns into worried me. I just can't help it. When everything's going fine with not even a wisp of a cloud in the sky, my imagination leaps in. I suddenly imagine all the things that could go wrong. And then I start to believe they actually will go wrong. And before you know it, I'm worrying.

Then Gran tells me, 'Don't look so worried. It'll probably never happen.' And most of the time she's right.

Trying Our Best

I tried to remember that now as I looked at the team's smiling faces.

They'd all worked so hard. I couldn't let them know how I was feeling. It wouldn't be fair.

'Brilliant work, everyone,' I said, and smiled too. Then the bell rang to end break time.

I sighed. *Even if we don't save Saint David's Day, I thought, at least we'll have tried our best.*

'You'd better start delivering those newspapers,' Sir said, as he strolled back into the classroom. 'All the teachers are expecting you. But be quick – Mrs Right's due back at lunchtime.'

'I'll do the nursery,' I told the others. I was still feeling worried about our plan. And when I feel worried I like to go back to the nursery.

'Fine,' they all said, and I headed off to see Miss Juno.

Miss Juno

Miss Juno wears long skirts, bright beads and jangly bangles. Her class smells of warm milk and biscuits. There are things made of wool and pipe cleaners hanging down from the ceiling. And things made of tin foil and drinking straws climbing up the walls. And there's sand and water and paint everywhere.

'Come in, come in,' she said when I knocked on her door. She has a floaty kind of voice, like one of those ladies at the fair who promise to tell your fortune. 'Come in to my Magical Wonderland.'

Miss Juno's Magical Wonderland

Miss Juno always calls her classroom her 'Magical Wonderland'. And to be fair, it does feel pretty magical when you're in there.

The tiny children in her class look just like pixies in little school uniforms. They only ever do things like painting,

singing songs and building sandcastles in the sandpit. They don't have to do any proper schoolwork, so that *is* pretty magical.

And when you go in there, you suddenly feel like you're four again. Sometimes that feels weird, and sometimes it feels good. Today it felt good. Very, very good.

'Ah, Seren Wen, I've been expecting you,' Miss Juno said, in her floaty voice. 'I remember when you were a little, little child.'

She says that to everyone – even Lucy. And she didn't move to Wales until she was nine.

Miss Juno shook the biscuit tin under my nose. 'I hear you come with good news.' She was peering at me with very twinkly eyes.

'You're saving Saint David's Day.'

'We hope so,' I said, taking a custard cream. 'We're hoping to have a brilliant concert this year.'

'Well, all the little ones in my class will dress up for the day,' she said. 'And instead of just one song, we'll learn three. And we'll do a dance too. How's that?'

'That'll be wonderful, Miss Juno.' I nibbled my biscuit.

'But you look sad, Seren Wen,' she said. 'Tell me, what's troubling you?'

Miss Juno's Prediction

That's the thing about Miss Juno – she can always tell when you're not feeling right.

I sighed. 'I'm afraid no one else will be interested,' I said. 'I'm afraid the concert will be a flop again, like last year.'

Miss Juno tapped my arm with a sparkly ringed finger. 'Have no fear. I predict this year's

concert will be the best ever.
Now, would you like to play
in the Wendy house?' And she
pointed to the little playhouse. It
was full of tiny children sitting on tiny chairs
playing with tiny cups and saucers. It all looked
very sweet.

'I'd love to,' I said, 'but I don't think I'd fit
through the door.'

'Ah,' Miss Juno sighed. 'How quickly my little
chicks grow up.'

'I'd better get back to my lessons,' I said. I was
feeling much better now. Visiting the nursery
had worked like a charm. 'Sir will be wondering
where I am.' And I waved goodbye to Miss Juno
and skipped all the way back to class.

Chapter 14

All On Board

Heroes

At lunchtime the *Seren Wen* team  got together again. We had a lot to report.

Dylan was first with his news.

'Mr Killer was really pleased with our plan. He called us all heroes. He said no one had the power to cancel Saint David's Day, not even Mrs Right.'

'That's what Mr Terry said too,' Lucy told us.

 'He was really mad that she didn't want to have a concert this year.'

'Mrs Biggs said the same,' added Nia.

'And Mrs Candy,' said Rob. 'She's going to teach her class two songs.'

Jac nodded. 'Mr Harry said the same thing.'

'Miss Juno said her class will do *three* songs this year,' I said. 'And a dance too. If everyone makes that kind of effort, we'll have a fantastic concert.'

And with that Andy Morris and his friends came running up.

The Soccer Lot

Andy and his friends are in Mr Harry's class and they're mad about soccer. They never do anything else if they can help it. And one of them is always carrying a football.

'We've just been reading the latest copy of *Seren Wen* over lunch,' Andy said. He was really excited. 'And we're getting a choir together for the concert. We're going to practise at lunchtimes. This Saint David's Day will be brilliant.'

He threw down his football and kicked it across the playground. His friends ran after it, pulling and pushing each other out of the way. 'Make the most of it,' he called to them. 'It's our last game for a week.' And then he dashed off too.

'I'm amazed,' Dylan said. 'Andy Morris is giving up soccer to sing in the school concert!'

'Wow,' I said.

And then Emily Sugarland ran up.

Emily's Song

'I was wondering if you'd all like to be in my choir,' Emily said. 'I'm writing a song for the concert.' She looked at us hopefully.

'Is it about unicorns?' Dylan asked gruffly. 'Or mermaids? I'm not singing a song about those.'

'It's about dragons, of course,' Emily said, 'because it's for Saint David's Day.'

'Oh, that's alright then.' Dylan smiled.

That's typical of my brother – he thinks mythical creatures like unicorns and mermaids are stupid, but dragons are absolutely fine.

'I'll be in your choir,' I told Emily. And the rest of the team nodded too.

'Great,' Emily said. 'See you for practice later.' And she skipped off.

'We've got lots of acts for the concert already,' I said. And just as I started to think our plan might work after all, Sneaky Sandra slithered round the corner.

What Now?

'What do *you* want?' Dylan asked her. I told you he can be blunt.

Sneaky Sandra sniggered. 'It says in your silly little newspaper that the Saint David's Day concert

is a surprise for Mrs Right. How much is that surprise worth?'

'What do you mean?' Jac asked.

'Well, if I say I'll go and tell her about it right now,' Sandra said, 'what will you give me not to?'

'I think you'll find that's blackmail,' Rob said. He sounded shocked.

'Exactly!' Sandra laughed.

We couldn't believe it – the cheek of the girl.

'Don't you want to save Saint David's Day?' Lucy asked.

'No, not really.' Sandra shrugged.

'Go and tell Mrs Right if you want,' Dylan told her. 'We're not paying you a penny.'

'OK,' she said. 'I will.' And she ran off towards the staffroom.

'Oh no.' I could have cried. 'That'll spoil

everything. Once Mrs Right finds out about the concert, she'll ruin our plan.'

But Rob patted my shoulder. 'Don't worry,' he said. 'I can fix this.' And he ran off on the trail of Sneaky Sandra.

Chapter 15

Rob to the Rescue Again

Mrs Right Returns

We couldn't just wait there doing nothing. 'Come on,' I said. 'Let's see what Rob's going to do.' And we followed him and Sandra into school.

We hung around the corridor near the staffroom. The front door opened with a bang and someone called 'I'm back!' It was Mrs Right. She's always shouting in the corridors. We're not allowed to, of course, but she does.

I peeked around the corner. Sneaky Sandra was waiting for Mrs Right outside the staffroom door. And Mrs Right was heading straight for her. 'Ah, Sandra,' she said, 'what can I do for you today?' There was no sign of Rob anywhere.

'There's going to be a concert,' Sandra started

to say. She always put on a very sweet voice when she spoke to Mrs Right. And Mrs Right fell for it every time. It was unbelievable. Why couldn't she see the sneakiness in Sneaky Sandra?

'A concert?' Mrs Right said.

Oh no, this was terrible. Where was Rob? If he didn't do something soon, Sandra would ruin everything.

'Yes,' Sandra said. 'And it's a surprise.'

'How lovely,' Mrs Right said. 'When is it?'

'It's on Saint —'

But before Sandra could finish, Rob charged around the corner.

Aeroplane Rob

He was pretending to be a plane. It's not the sort of thing Rob normally does – honest. But we guessed it was part of his plan. And he was making as much noise as he could.

Mrs Right forgot about Sneaky Sandra. 'Robert Roberts!' she said in an extremely loud voice. 'Stop that noise at once. And stop running in the corridor.'

We watched Rob skid to a halt next to the staffroom door.

'You seem to be everywhere I turn,' she carried on. 'Tying up your shoe-laces outside my office and knocking over bins.' Then she turned to Sandra. 'Enjoy the concert you were telling me about. Have fun. Now off you go outside, both of you.' And she went into the staffroom and closed the door.

Sneaky Sandra looked at Rob. 'Don't think you've won,' she said.

'I'll get lots of chances to tell Mrs Right what you're up to.'

Rob smiled. 'And I will be around every corner, just waiting to ruin your nasty little plan.'

'Hummph,' Sandra snorted. And off she stormed. She knew she'd never get the better of Rob. He's far too good at sleuthing.

It's All Going to Plan – Phew!

By the end of lunchtime my head was spinning. The *Seren Wen* team hadn't had a minute's peace since we'd finished dinner. After Andy told us

about his choir plan and Emily asked us about her song, Luke, Ben and Celyn said they were planning a dance routine. Then Mr Killer sent us a note to say his class were writing a poem called 'The Wonders of Wales'. I didn't need to worry after all. Everyone in school wanted to save Saint David's Day and I breathed a sigh of relief.

Mrs Right had enjoyed her computer course. All afternoon she kept popping her head into our classroom to say things like, 'I know exactly where the delete key is now, but I'm not going to press it unless I really need to.' And, 'Caps Lock is very useful, isn't it? I think I might keep it on all the time.'

But she didn't mention a thing about Saint David's Day. It was clear she hadn't read the latest copy of *Seren Wen*. And no one had told her about it either, not even Sneaky Sandra.

Oh No, More Worries

I should have been feeling very happy, but by the end of the day I had more worries. I told you I turned into a worrier, didn't I? Remember that imagination of mine? Well, it was running riot and I couldn't stop it.

What if we had too many people doing things? What if we didn't have time for them all? What if we had hundreds of choirs and hundreds of dances and hundreds of people telling us poems? How would we cope? The concert was only meant to last one afternoon, not all week!

A Worry Shared is a Worry Solved

While I was putting away my books and quietly worrying to myself, Nia and Lucy came over to my desk.

'Everything OK, Seren Wen?' Nia asked. 'You look a bit worried. Aren't you pleased with what we've done today?' Nia's good at working

out how people are feeling. That's why she does the interviews for our paper.

'Oh, I know we've worked really hard,' I said. 'And it's so great that everyone's going to help, but …' I sighed. 'What if too many people want to be in the concert? How will we fit them all in?'

'I was wondering about that too,' Lucy said. And she opened her bag and got out a sheet of paper with lots of lines and times on it. 'I thought we'd better get organised, so I've drawn up a timetable for the concert, and I've given each class fifteen minutes. That'll mean the concert lasts two hours. What do you think?'

And then I remembered one of Gran's favourite sayings – a worry shared is a worry halved.

Or solved in this case. Lucy is very practical. She's the one who does puzzles and crosswords for *Seren Wen*. I should have known that she could solve my problem.

'I think a timetable is a brilliant idea. It's just

 what we need,' I said. 'Thanks, Lucy.' And I gave her a huge smile.

Chapter 16

Full Steam Ahead

Filling Up the Timetable

The *Seren Wen* team got to school early again the next day. We met in our favourite place in the playground – round the corner by the tool shed. I showed everyone the timetable Lucy had made and they all agreed it was a great idea. We began filling it in.

'Loads of people have already signed up for the concert,' Dylan said. 'We only need a few more and the timetable will be full.'

'How many people want to enter the baking competition, Jac?' I asked.

'Masses,' he said. 'And Sir has promised to judge it.'

We all nodded. We knew Sir would agree to taste the Welsh cakes. He never refuses any food – ever. He'd make the perfect judge for a baking competition.

'He was really excited when I asked him,' Jac said. 'But so many people are entering. I think he might be biting off more than even he can chew.'

'I'm sure he'll cope,' Dylan said. 'Remember that time Mrs Right brought cream cakes to school?' And everyone nodded.

The Cream Cake Catastrophe

One morning before school started, Mrs Right was going past the bakers in town. She likes to talk to lots of people, so she went in for a chat. Then she saw they were selling cream cakes for half the normal price. Mrs Right can never resist a bargain – remember the lime green paint? So she bought twenty cakes. Twenty great big buns full of swirly fresh cream. But when she got to school she forgot all about the cakes and left them in her car.

At lunchtime she remembered. 'Oh no,' she cried. 'It's a catastrophe!' And she ran out to get them. But it was too late. The sun had been warming the cakes all morning and the cream tasted yucky. Nobody wanted to eat them.

Nobody, that is, except Sir. He thought they tasted fine. And since no one else wanted any, he finished them all off. Twenty of them! We know, because Sir told us about it when he got back to class.

He was quite proud. But his face did look very green, and he had to keep running back and fore to the toilet all afternoon.

Back in the Playground

'I'm sure a hundred Welsh cakes won't be too much for Sir,' Dylan said. 'He could probably

manage a thousand if he had to.'
And with that the bell rang for
the start of school.

Mrs Right was waiting for us as we lined up
to go inside. 'Don't go to your classes,' she said.
'Go straight to the hall for assembly. I've got
something important to tell you all.'

We weren't surprised. Sir had already told
us that Mrs Right was going to make an
announcement in assembly, remember? She
was going to tell us that Saint David's Day was
cancelled. She was going to say that it would be
an ordinary day this year. She was going to tell
us that there wouldn't be a concert.

'Here we go,' I said to Dylan, as we filed into
the hall. 'She's going to break the news about
cancelling the concert.'

'Yeah,' he agreed. 'Not that it matters now.
We all know it's going ahead anyway.'

And we felt quite pleased with ourselves.

Mrs Right's Surprise

'This year,' Mrs Right began, 'there will be no Saint David's Day concert.'

Nobody said anything. We all just sat there looking at her. Everyone was expecting it. We had told them in the paper that she would be making this announcement.

'Well, you're all very quiet,' she said, peering at us. 'I can see you're not at all bothered.' She looked at the teachers. They were sitting in a row at the back of the hall. 'You see. I told you the children wouldn't mind if I cancelled Saint David's Day.'

The teachers didn't say a word either. We were all feeling quite smug. The whole school had a plan to save Saint David's Day. And Mrs Right was the only person who didn't know it.

'I was going to say we would have lessons as usual,' she said. 'But instead, I thought I would arrange a treat for you.' And she began skipping about and singing the words 'treat for you' over and over. I told you she liked singing and dancing in her assemblies, remember?

A treat? I thought. *A treat?* Oh no, what could she mean? And then she dropped her bombshell.

Chapter 17

Mrs Right
Ruins Everything

The Bombshell

'I've asked Reverend Right to come and speak to the whole school,' she said. 'His talk will be called "The History of Wales Through the Ages."' And she smiled at us all, as if she was giving us a huge present. 'You lucky things.'

Suddenly everyone started talking at once.

'Yes, yes, I know it's exciting,' Mrs Right said, 'but quieten down now.' She thought we were excited about the Reverend's visit.

But I knew what everyone was saying – if Reverend

Right was giving one of his talks, how would we have time for a concert? We all knew that his talks go on for ages. *Ages.*

And *aaages.*

Reverend Right

Reverend Right is Mrs Right's husband. He comes into school once a week for assembly and

his talks are always very boring. But we don't mind too much because he's funny. Well, *he*'s not funny. His false teeth are.

He's got false teeth because he ate too many sweets when he was a boy. He told us in one very long assembly. And he said he didn't brush his teeth very well either, so the dentist said he had to have false ones. And the false ones rattle around his mouth when he talks. Every now and again they almost fall out. And when he's excited, if you're

very lucky, they *do* fall out. Someone in the front row has to dodge them. Reverend Right doesn't care. He just says 'Now where did my teeth go?' But it's hard to understand him, because he hasn't got his teeth in. Then he just picks them up off the floor, gives them a wipe on his sleeve and pops them back in his mouth.

And you don't really mind how long he talks for, because there's always a chance his teeth might fall out again.

But if he came on Saint David's Day, there would be no way we could have a concert. He would talk and talk and talk until the bell went for home time. And it wouldn't matter how many times his teeth fell out, it wouldn't be funny. Because our plans would be ruined.

And so would Saint David's Day.

Down in the Dumps

Everyone was asking the same question at break time – what are we going to do? And who were they asking? Me, of course. Sensible me. And I didn't have any answers because, like I told you, I'm *not* sensible. People just think I am. It's hard being me sometimes. I wished I hadn't thought up a plan for saving Saint David's Day. I wished Rob hadn't seen the question mark on Mrs Right's calendar. I was beginning to wish I'd never even started the newspaper in the first place.

I wanted to run away and hide. But instead I looked at the rest of the *Seren Wen* team and said, 'We need to brainstorm. Now!'

'We could lock Reverend Right out of school,' Nia suggested.

Lucy shook her head. 'Mrs Right would just open the door and let him in.'

'We could kidnap him,' Jac said. 'Tie him up in a cupboard.'

Rob shook his head this time. 'I think you'll

find kidnapping is against the law.'

Dylan shrugged. 'We could distract him. He's very easy to distract.'

And then I remembered something. 'That's brilliant, Dylan,' I said. 'That's exactly what we'll do.'

Rocks and Cakes

What I remembered was this – Reverend Right likes rocks. I know because he gave us a long talk about them once. And his teeth fell out three times in that assembly. He was *very* excited. And he also likes cakes. I know because he always has cake crumbs on his cardigan. Always.

Rocks and cakes. It's a bit of a random thought, I know. But it'll make sense, you'll see. I asked myself 'Who else likes rocks and cakes?' even though I already knew the answer. And the answer was – Sir.

When we went back into class after break, I headed for his desk. 'Seren Wen,' he said, 'just the person I wanted to talk to. All the teachers have been asking me what we're going to do about Reverend Right.

Are we cancelling Saint David's Day after all?'

I shook my head firmly. 'No, Sir. Not if we can help it. We've got another plan.'

'Great,' Sir said. 'I knew you'd think of something.'

And then I told him about my plan. 'Do you think you can do it, Sir?' I asked.

'No problem,' he said with a smile. 'No problem at all.'

Chapter 18

Mrs Right Ruins Everything – Again!

Daffodils and Leeks

The first of March was bright and sunny. Walking to school that morning was weird and wonderful. Everywhere you looked there were people in Welsh costume. There were tall black hats and

small black bonnets. The boys were wearing flat caps, and they had leeks and daffodils on their waistcoats. And everyone was carrying tins  full of cakes for the baking competition. It was fantastic. Even Sneaky Sandra and Sneaky Sid had a plastic tub each full of Welsh cakes.

'What on earth will Mrs Right say when she sees us all?' Lucy said, as she ran to catch up with Dylan and me.

'I think she'll be sorry she cancelled the concert,' I said.

But when we got to school, there was no sign of Mrs Right.

'Her car wouldn't start this morning,' Sir told us. 'She won't be in until later. I promised her I'd hold the fort. And I told her that she wouldn't believe her eyes when she got here.'

He was right. She wouldn't believe her eyes. And she wouldn't believe how hard everyone had been practising their songs, poems and dances either. But she'd find out in the afternoon. As long as she made it to school by then.

All for Nothing

By the start of lunchtime, her car still hadn't turned up in the car park.

'What are we going to do if she doesn't come?' Nia asked. 'The whole school thinks Saint David's Day is special. But if Mrs Right's not here for our concert, we'll have done all that work for nothing. And she won't know how we feel.'

'It's such a shame,' Jac moaned.

'We've got ten tables covered with cakes in our classroom, and she's not even going to see them.'

We all looked gloomy.

Then Rob ran up. 'I have important information.' He opened his notebook and started reading.

'At exactly oh twelve hundred hours and …' He stopped. 'At exactly oh *one* hundred hours and …' He stopped again.

'Forget about the twenty-four hour clock for now, Rob,' I told him.

'OK then,' he said. 'Two minutes ago, I overheard Mr Morgan, known to us as Sir, talking to Mrs Right on the telephone. "So your car's been repaired, Reverend Right is driving you to school, and we'll see you in time for the concert." That's what Sir said.'

'The concert?' I gasped. 'Did he actually say the word "concert"?'

'He did indeed,' Rob said. 'But Sir corrected himself quickly. "The talk" he said, "I meant the Reverend's talk" and then he hung up.'

I bit my lip. 'Let's hope she doesn't know what we're up to.

It's nearly time for the concert to start.' I looked at the excited faces of the *Seren Wen* team and tried my best to smile. 'Fingers crossed, everyone.'

Destruct Reverend Right

By the time the bell rang for the start of the afternoon, the whole school was sitting in the hall ready for the concert. Through the window we saw a little red car drive into the car park. Out got Mrs Right and the Reverend, and they chatted away as they walked to the front door. They were talking so much they didn't notice everyone sitting quietly in the hall.

I nodded at Sir. He nodded back and stood up. He knew what he had to do. 'OK,' he whispered to me. 'I'm going to put your "Destruct Reverend Right" plan into operation.'

'My what?' I asked.

'Your "Destruct Reverend Right" plan,' he said. 'Destruct him with rocks and cakes, like you told me.'

'No.' I shook my head firmly. 'Not destruct – *distract*. You're meant to *distract* him with your film about rocks. You know – the one you filmed when you broke your ankle and you were waiting for the air ambulance. And you're meant to feed him Welsh cakes too.'

Sir nodded his head. 'Oh yes, I remember now,' he said. 'Distract not destruct. Distract not destruct.' And off he went.

Then Mrs Right burst into the hall.

A Surprise for Mrs Right

'Oh my goodness,' she exclaimed when she saw our Welsh costumes. 'I'd forgotten it was Saint David's Day today. You all look so wonderful in your costumes. I wish we had a concert planned now. But Reverend Right is here instead and he's going to give you a very interesting talk indeed.'

And then she turned and looked behind her for the Reverend, but he had disappeared. Sir had already led him away, with the promise of a film about rocks and as many Welsh cakes as he could eat.

I cleared my throat and stood up. My knees were shaking and I felt very embarrassed, but if I didn't say it nobody else would.

'Actually, Mrs Right,' I said, trying to make my voice as loud as I could, 'we've got a surprise for you.'

And with that Miss Juno started bashing away at the piano. The nursery class climbed up onto the stage. And the most wonderful Saint David's Day concert that our school has ever seen began.

Chapter 19

Would Our Plan Work?

Absolutely Amazing!

It was fantastic. There were so many songs and dances, and almost no one forgot the words to their poems. The nursery children danced and sang their tiny hearts out and Mr Killer's class recited the poem they'd written called 'The Wonders of Wales'. It had lines about puffins and dolphins, and red kites and snowy nights, and train rides and mountainsides and lots more too. Andy's soccer team choir nearly took the roof off with their version of 'Bread of Heaven'. And Luke, Celyn and Ben's body-popping dance to a speeded-up Welsh folk tune was absolutely amazing.

The afternoon just flew by. The teachers gave out the prizes, and even Emily Sugarland won a book for her song about dragons. The *Seren Wen* team had done a pretty good job of singing it, even if I say so myself. And Emily was very pleased with her prize.

'A book about fairies!' she said. 'Just what I wanted!'

A Shock for Sneaky Sandra

Finally Sir came back into the hall. Reverend Right was following him. His cardigan was covered in crumbs.

'The Reverend and I,' Sir told the school, 'have spent a most enjoyable afternoon tasting Welsh cakes.' He hiccupped loudly. 'And we have decided that the Best Baking prize goes to …' He looked around the hall.

Everyone held their breath.

'Sid Dreary.'

We all clapped as Sid went up to get his prize. But I saw Sneaky Sandra scowling. She didn't like Sid to be better than her at anything.

I looked at Dylan. 'Wow,' I said, 'Sneaky Sid is good at cooking. Who'd have thought it?'

Lucy tapped my arm. 'That's everything on the timetable finished. Are you going to say something to end the concert?'

I hadn't thought of that. I was hoping that Sir might say something, but he was too full of cake. And his hiccups had got really loud.

So I stood up, even though my knees were very wobbly, and I turned to face Mrs Right.

My Speech

'We hope you enjoyed our Saint David's Day concert,

Mrs Right,' I said. My knees were shaking and my voice was too. 'As you can see, everyone made a very big effort.' I waved my arm at the people in the hall. 'We all wore Welsh costumes, and we all learned a new piece to perform. We did that because our national day is very special to us.'

I could see lots of heads nodding. Everyone was agreeing with me. So I took a big breath and I carried on. 'I promise that we'll keep it special – every single year.' My knees were really wobbling now. 'So please, Mrs Right,' I said, in my best pleading voice, 'please don't cancel Saint David's Day again.'

There was silence. No one dared breathe. Even Sir's hiccups had stopped. My legs were wobbling so much I was sure I would fall over. What would Mrs Right say?

We waited.

And we waited.

Mrs Right's Reply

Mrs Right cleared her throat. She looked at us, and we looked at her.

'I've never seen such a wonderful concert,' she said finally, and her voice was as wobbly as my legs. She got a tissue from her pocket and dabbed her eyes. 'The surprise you've given me today has been fantastic. You've really shown me how much Saint David's Day means to you.' She took a deep breath. 'I promise I will never, *ever* cancel it again.'

We gasped. She'd said it. She'd promised never to cancel it again. She had. She had!

Job Done

Everyone started cheering. It had worked. Our plan had actually worked. The *Seren Wen* team waved our arms in the air. We grinned at each other.

'We did it,' I said. 'We actually saved Saint David's Day.'

I slumped down into my seat. My legs were shaking too much to hold me up any more.

'Great job, sis,' Dylan said, patting my back. He had to shout it because of the cheering. Sir had started hiccupping again and Nia, Jac, Rob and Lucy were still jumping around and punching the air. We were all grinning and grinning.

'Thanks, bro,' I said.

And then I heard him say something else. He said it really quietly so it was hard to hear over all the noise in the hall.

'Wow, Dylan Siôn,' I said. 'Did you just say you were proud of me?'

Dylan looked at me in amazement. 'What?' he said. 'You're kidding! All this newspaper business must be going to your head.'

And then he laughed.

Very loudly.

Isn't that just typical of my brother? Just typical!

'Yeah,' I said. 'I thought I must be wrong. I knew you'd never say something that nice to me.'

And then I started laughing too.